VOLUME

EIGHT

IMAGE COMICS, INC.

www.imagecomics.com

SAGA, VOLUME EIGHT. First printing. December 2017. Published by Image Comics, Inc. Office of publication: 2701 NW Vaughn St, Suite 780, Portland, OR 97210. Copyright © 2017 Brian K. Vaughan & Fiona Staples. Originally published in single magazine form as SAGA #43–48. All rights reserved. SAGA, its logos, and all character likenesses herein are trademarks of Brian K. Vaughan & Fiona Staples unless otherwise noted. "Image" and the Image Comics logos are registered trademarks of Image Comics, Inc. No part of this publication may be reproduced or transmitted, in any form or by any means (except for short excerpts for journalistic or review purposes), without the express written permission of Brian K. Vaughan, Fiona Staples, or Image Comics, Inc. All names, characters, events, and locales in this publication are entirely fictional. Any resemblance to actual persons (living or dead), events or places, without satiric intent, is coincidental. Printed in the USA. For information regarding the CPSIA on this printed material call: 203-595-3636 and provide reference # RICH–767569. ISBN 978-1-5343-0349-2

FOR INTERNATIONAL RIGHTS, CONTACT: foreignlicensing@imagecomics.com

FIONA STAPLES
ARTIST

BRIAN K. VAUGHAN
WRITER

FONOGRAFIKS
LETTERING + DESIGN

ERIC STEPHENSON
COORDINATOR

CHAPTER FORTY-THREE

WELCOME TO
ABORTION TOWN!
Howdy, strangers.

A very pleasant morning to you, Doctor Sheriff.
My name is Earl Robot LI, and I was hoping you good people would be able to assist one of my young soldiers with her... situation.

Well, I'll be. We don't get much royalty this far out west.
But of course, we're here to help *all* women in their time of need.
Thank you.

Sorry, sir. Gonna have to ask you to stay *outside* city limits.
Abortion Town is only for ladies and their immediate family.
Ma'am, this gentleman *is* family.

He's the father of my child.

But... I didn't think his kind and... and wings could... you know...

We were under the same belief, but let me assure you that procreation between our races is unquestionably possible.
Still, our unplanned offspring will likely suffer horrific mutations, so for the good of both our worlds, we need the fetus terminated and its remains *discreetly* disposed of.

Huh.
How far along are you, darling?
Um, about eight months.

Your third trimester?
I'm powerful sorry... but there ain't a thing we can do for you.

I beg your fucking pardon.

Simmer down, Earl.
Wish it weren't the case, but we're under Landfall jurisdiction.
You don't like their rules for a woman's body, you can take it up with the wings' elected officials... most of whom ain't women, mind you.

This isn't about your utterly banal political sentiments, this is about our lives.
Please, we came as soon as we could, but we were very far away from the only planet that offers this... procedure.
Isn't there anything you can do?

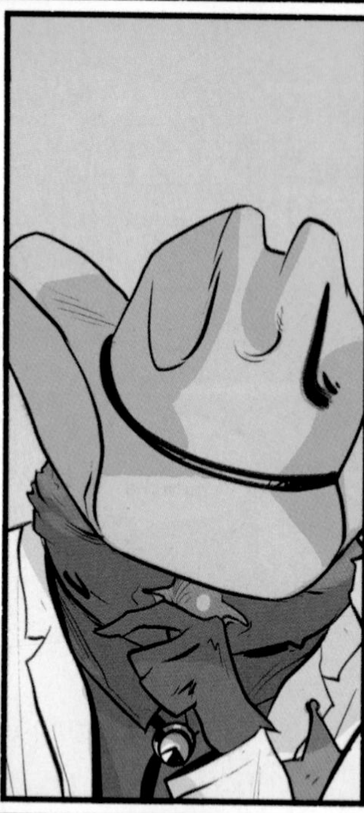

On the other side of this rock, there's a place called the Badlands.
Hell of a dangerous trip, but the "doctors" out that way are willing to do just about anything, no questions asked.

But y'all didn't hear that from me.

Never fear, Alana.
No matter how long it takes, we will journey to these Badlands and finish what --

We aren't doing shit, Sir Robot.
The only reason I let you tag along is so we could try this stupid ruse of yours... and now that it's predictably gone tits up, you and I are finished.

But... where am I supposed to go?
I don't give a good goddamn.
All I know is I never want to see your face again.

My name's Hazel, and this is my mother.
But that's not me in there, and this is definitely not my father.

It's kind of a long story, but I can get you up to speed.

In the beginning, there was Landfall and there was Wreath.
Landfall, the planet where Mom was born, is a restless sci-fi wonderland, always bulldozing over its past to put up something shinier.
BLACK 2.1
today

Wreath, Dad's home moon, is a magical fantasy realm rooted in ancient tradition, pretty much the OPPOSITE of the world it orbits.

Despite what you may have heard, opposites NEVER attract.

In time, this endless war spread far beyond where it began, forcing everyone in the universe to choose between the wings and the horns.

Somehow, these two oddballs never got the memo.

In the years since they both went AWOL from their respective militaries, my parents had plenty of adventures...

... including making ME.
Why are you crying?
Is my little brother okay?

But there are few things more challenging than a sequel.
No, my heart.
Mommy got hurt and we... I'm afraid we *lost* him.
Is everyone all right?

I was just about to kick this worthless drone out the front hatch.
Still, if there's one thing I learned from the unlikely allies we made over the years, it's that family is about much more than blood.

Petrichor, what... what happened to your hands?

She sacrificed her own flesh to launch us to safety.
You owe this woman an extraordinary debt of --
Shut your filthy screen, you manipulative little...

Snf
Snf

Sankta vazo.

I am blessed to be in your presence, Most Holy Mother.

What the hell is this?
Petri, he's **gone**. My baby is --
Some faiths on Wreath **revere** women who have suffered... what **we** just have.

Your wife is no longer a mere "*woman*," Marko.
Anyone carrying the remains of an unborn Wreath child is a ***sacred vessel***.
Bullshit.

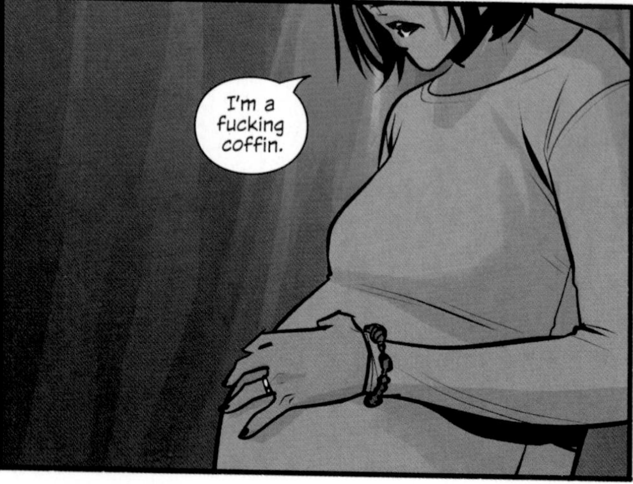
I'm a fucking coffin.

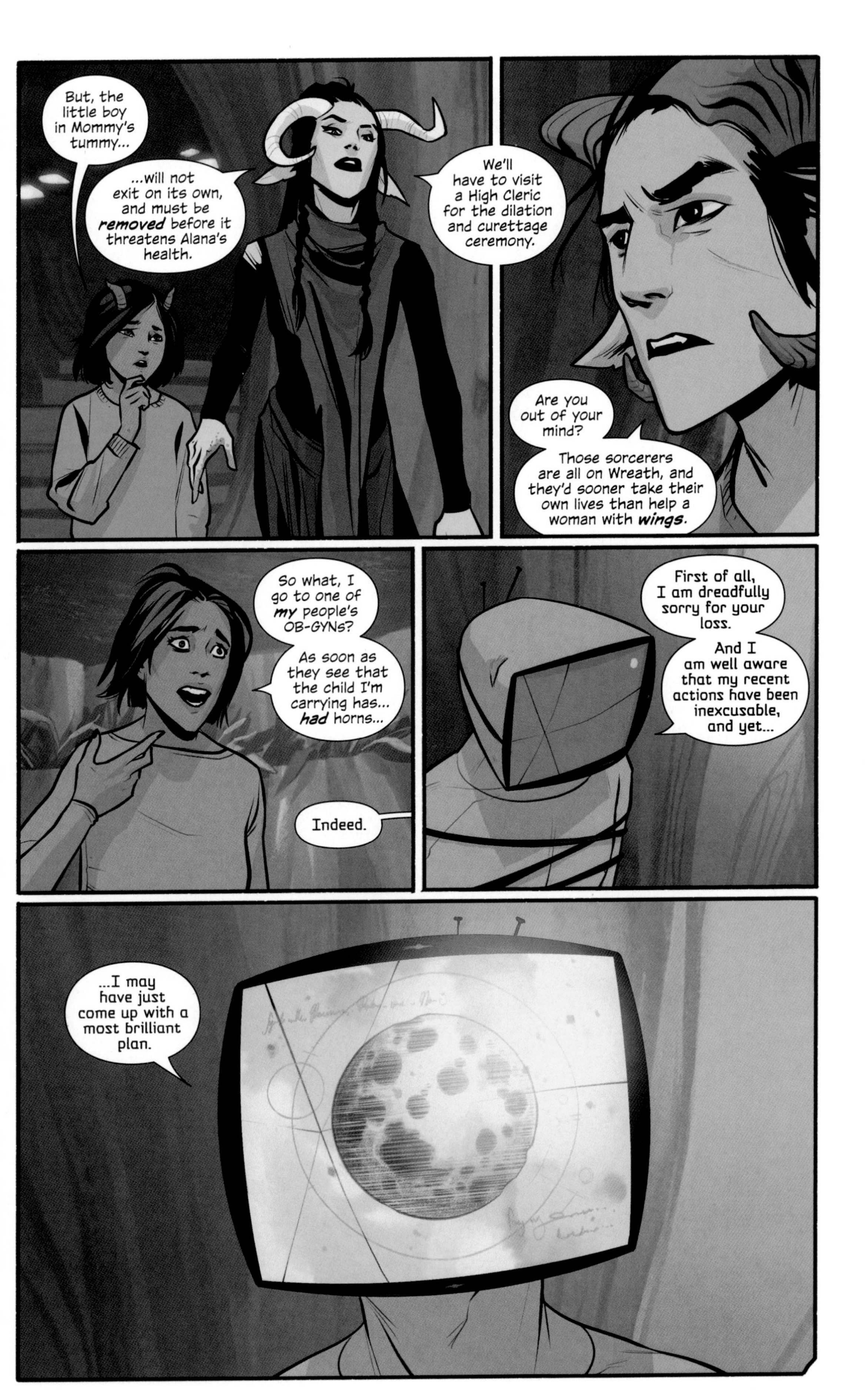
But, the little boy in Mommy's tummy...
...will not exit on its own, and must be *removed* before it threatens Alana's health.
We'll have to visit a High Cleric for the dilation and curettage ceremony.
Are you out of your mind?
Those sorcerers are all on Wreath, and they'd sooner take their own lives than help a woman with *wings*.
So what, I go to one of *my* people's OB-GYNs?
As soon as they see that the child I'm carrying has... *had* horns...
Indeed.
First of all, I am dreadfully sorry for your loss.
And I am well aware that my recent actions have been inexcusable, and yet...
...I may have just come up with a most brilliant plan.

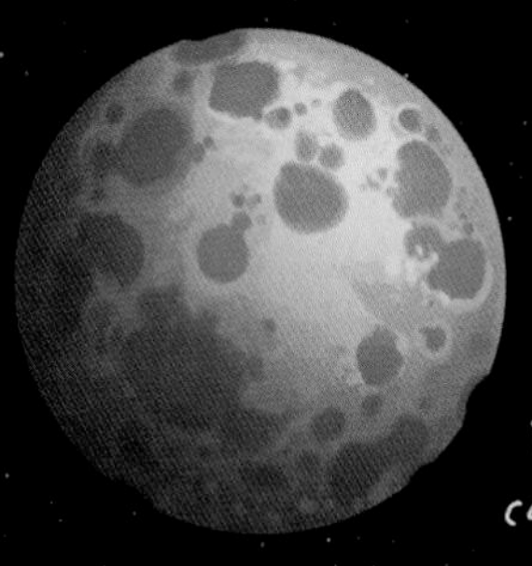
And that's how we ended up here, somewhere inside an outpost planet called PERVIOUS.

After a brutal few months for us, this was a time of healing and recovery.

But some folks bounce back faster than others.

Ow!

Oops, sorry, Petrichor.
You're doing fine, little one.
Just tie my dressings as tight as you can.

You sure you don't want my dad to do this?
Marko is busy making a new septic line to remove the waste from your rocketship.
Waste? Like, pee and poop? I thought we just flush that stuff out when we're in space.

As did I.
Then, why has he been digging like that all week?
You're asking the wrong person. I'll ***never*** understand why men do the things they do.

That reminds me.
Can I ask about your penis?

You most certainly may not.
Because what you learned when we were imprisoned together is *private*.
Oh. But, how come?
More importantly, I refuse to be defined by my genitalia.
When you question the biology of some-one who happens to be transgender, you don't just objectify us, you make us feel illegitimate and...

What in the world is the matter?
I didn't mean to hurt your feelings, Petrichor.
I'm just... super, super scared.

Of what?
I, I, I have wings like Mommy, but also horns like Daddy.
But, but, but I have girl parts in my swimsuit places, and I don't know if maybe I'll grow boy parts next. What if everything in my body goes wrong and I *die*?
Ah.

I just wish... I just wish I was normal.
Little one, you are unlike anyone who has ever existed, and that makes you *exactly* like everyone who has ever existed.
I don't know what the future holds for you or your body...

...but I promise that you will never be alone.

Also, can I ask you a question about nipples?
Er...

Hey, look!
Mommy's back!
Oh, thank God.

Whoa.
Easy now, Button.
Alana!

How did it go, my love?
It didn't.
I was too far along for the powers that be, but at least they pointed me in the direction of this planet's creepy back-alley option.

Wherever it is, I'm coming with you.
Not with those horns, you're not. This is still Landfall territory. You need to stay with Hazel here on the outskirts.
But there are ways for us to travel inconspicuously and --
I appreciate the offer, handsome, but this is something I need to finish on my own.
I can't let you do that, Alana.
Not when this is all my fault.

Hey, it took **both** of us to make this happen.
And there's nobody to blame for our pregnancy ending but a shitty universe that's cruel and random.
Violence always has a cost, and we lost this child because of the life *I* took.

What, that mercenary douche you killed on Phang?
Marko, we'd **all** be dead if you hadn't done what you did.

...maybe.
I'll just never understand why war is easy, and peace is so god-damn hard.
Mommy!

Are you all better now?
Where's Sir Robot?
Oh, he... he needed to keep moving, honey. His **son** is still out there, so he decided to--

Behind you!

OH, FUCKING!

Hazel, that's not a nice word, remember?
And you're still using it wrong.
What **are** those things?!

Dung People.
Some kinda microbes in the soil that animate **feces**, turn it into a gross approximation of whoever shat it out.

I accidentally made one the first time I got stuck digging trenches for my platoon to crap in.
You used to get latrine duty, too?
That's how my first commander would punish me for --

SQUACK

Marko!
VNNAX
Your planet's garbage weapons are useless against these monsters!
We need proper spellcasting to --
gwuhl
Mommy!
They're gonna make us all dead!
Like hell, baby.
Here's the thing about miscarriages.

They are painful, they are horrific, and they are very, very common.
There are no funerals for Those Who Might Have Been, leaving parents to mourn their loss in strange and unexpected ways.
But while a miscarriage may feel like the end of the world...

...it's actually just the beginning of a new one.
Wait, what?

end chapter forty-three

CHAPTER

FORTY-FOUR

"I'm allergic to condoms," he says.
"I promise I'll pull out," he says.
Fucking let it go, will you?
Yeah, look where that got us.
You think this is fun for me?
I used up every last day of leave I had left to tag along to this suck-ass planet.
Partner, there's a ***tax*** on bad-mouthin' my home.

And I intend to collect.

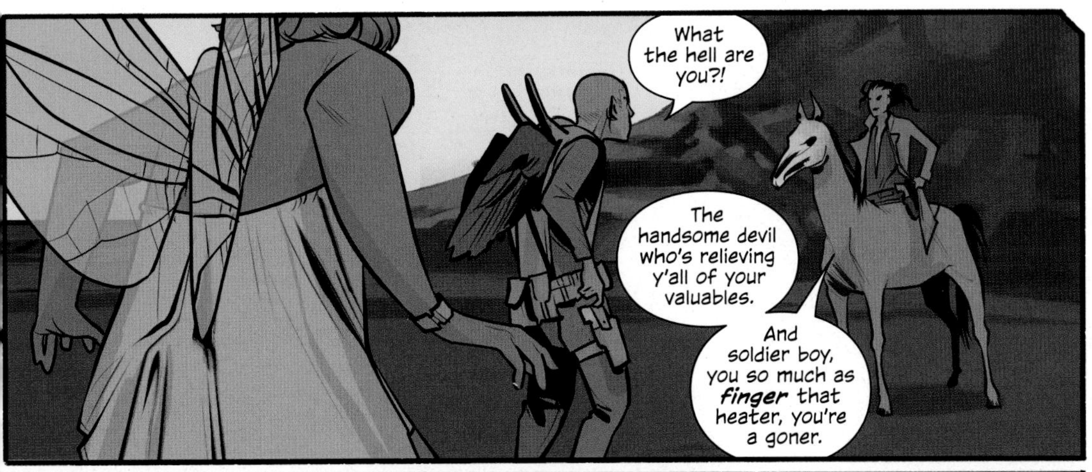
What the hell are you?!
The handsome devil who's relieving y'all of your valuables.
And soldier boy, you so much as *finger* that heater, you're a goner.

Try me, you sick --

KA-BLAM!

ROBIN!
Mighty sorry you had to see that, ma'am.
I really did try to --

RAHHH!

KABRAM

Bad form, Kidd.
Sexist to presume the girl didn't have a piece, too.

Dammit, Maw.
That lady was ***with child***.
Not for long. Wicked creature was about to have that poor baby ripped right out of her womb.

Just like them evil doctors told me I should do to ***you***.
Enough jawin'.

Either of you notice these *tracks*?

Probably just other bandits, Paw.
Nah, these belong to a well-heeled gentleman.
And him and his boots were headed *west*.

Nothing out there but the valley.
Why would outsiders risk comin' all the way to Pervious... only to move *away* from those Abortion Town butchers?
Decent question, son.

What say we go find the answer?
Every culture in the universe has a very different opinion about exactly when life begins.

But we're all pretty much in agreement on when it's over.

This is so weird.

No, it's *impossible*. Spells can only be cast by those with Wreath blood.
Obviously, when the child you two conceived... passed, it must have transferred its capabilities to Alana.
So can Mommy make bad guys' heads explode?!

Hazel, we've talked about this.
No matter what mistakes you've seen your daddy make, violence -- magical or otherwise -- is never acceptable.
Nonsense, Marko.
Violence is often ***essential***: in self-defense, the arts, foreplay...
I want to four-play!
I feel stronger... but also weaker.
God, it's like being pregnant all over ag--
GHWARR
That settles it.
We have to get that fetus out before it kills you.

I told you, ***I'll*** take care of it. This world isn't safe for your kind, Marko.
It's not safe for either of us ***anywhere*** in this universe, love.
But we've always been better off together.

What about me?!
Please, wherever you guys are going, I have to come with you!

She's right. This isn't the time to be splitting your nuclear family.
Besides, I already whipped up attire that should help conceal Hazel and Marko's modest horns.
"Modest?"

No offense, Petrichor, but why should I believe you won't just blast off with our rocket the second we leave you alone?
Because I'd like my ***sewing hands*** back before I take leave of you people.
If I hold down your fort, perhaps you'll inquire about a ***healing elixir*** for me from whatever quacks you find to perform your operation.

In that case, I'll leave you with ***this***.

You're giving her your ***wedding band***?
Is this some kind of kinky thrupple thing?
Because I'm not necessarily opposed.

I'm lending Petri one of our ***translation rings***.
If she runs into trouble with any of the locals, it'll at least give her a chance to talk her way out of it.

"*Talk.*"
Hilarious.

I agree, everything about this is ***ridiculous***.
We're all just gonna put on matching cowboy hats and ***hope*** that'll be enough to let us prance across the Badlands unscathed?

Who said anything about prancing?

A choo-choo.
A choo-choo **for real**.

That's an old Coalition model.
I spotted it while you and Sir Robot were in town.
Guards?
Only on the return route. It must pick them up with whatever laser-powder your people have them hauling out.

Which means the cars headed there are all **empty**.
That's the good news.
The bad is that this thing never stops, which means we'll have to board a **speeding train**.

It won't be easy, but if my calculations are correct, and we time things just right, we have a decent shot at --

Hold tight, baby.
We jump on three.

One.
Two.
Girls, wait!

WHEEEEEEEEEE!

Forgive me, Dad.

I had no idea how hard your job was.

Uhn!

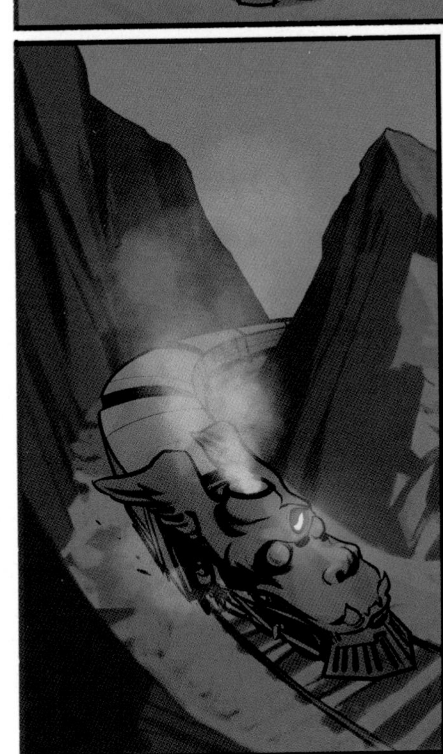

MARKO!

Fadenoj!

What she said!

hnnf

Mommy?
Yeah, sweetheart?
After they take out the dead baby, will Daddy put a new one in your tummy?

I... I don't know, Hazel.
We'll see, okay?
Every kid who's ever had a parent knows exactly what "we'll see" means.

Play your cards right,
and it's a sixty percent
chance of YES.

I've held you in my heart since the day you left me.

But you're too heavy to carry another step.

And I need to keep moving.

Saints above, I beseech you.

In all my years, I've asked for nothing.
But if you feel I've lived a decent life, hear this, my one and only prayer.

Please.
Send me someone to fuck.

Petri, you are a pathetic old hag, and you deserve to die alone.

It's a Wreather, all right.

A real one?
You're sure, Paw?
The hell is one of them doing in wing country?

Dunno.
But looks like she can spell something fierce.
Okay then.

Best do her before she can do us.

Whether we like it or not, most of our deepest-held beliefs come straight from the people who made us.

Even when we turn against them, our parents still help define exactly what kind of "rebels" we'll be.

Don't stop, I'm so close.
Yeah, suck my clit hard...

Hey, Alana.
You ever think about having *kids*?

What the fuck, Heath?
We've only been dating for, like, three weeks!
I don't mean having them with me! I mean, not necessarily. Just, you know, in general?

Dude, can you **picture** me with a baby?
Even my best friends say I'm a selfish bitch.

Actually, I think you'd be a great mother.
Also, the fact that you're a **junky**.
Well, my empty bank account and the last three houseplants I killed tell a different story.

What did you say?
You still dream about getting high on Fadeaway every single night, don't you?
I... I've never even tried that shit.

But you will.

No.
That's probably why you **miscarried**, right?
Because of all that **poison** you put into your body when Hazel was little.

You're a goddamn drug addict, and you **killed** your baby boy.

No.
It was an **accident**. It was just a...

...*mn?*

Oh.

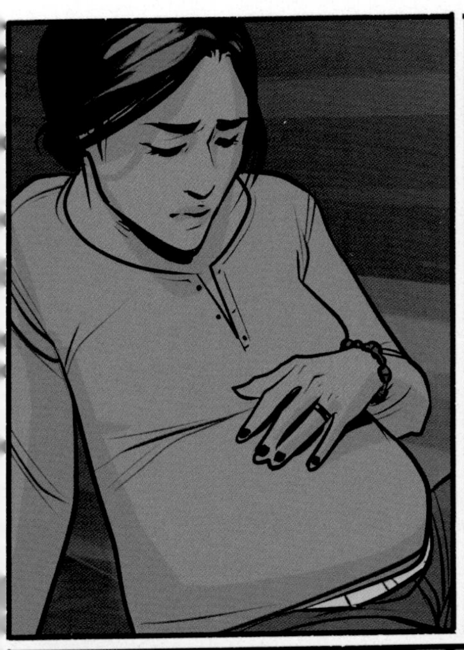

I don't deserve you.

Mom?
Sorry if I woke you, Hazel.
Mommy just had a bad dream.

"Hazel"?

I'm your **son,** silly.

end chapter forty-four

CHAPTER FORTY-FIVE

D. OSWALD
HEIST
PETITE DEATHS
Get your ass out here, moon woman!

Before we torch your dumb wooden ship and **smoke** you out!
OSWALD
HEIST
PETITE DEATHS
II

This is your last warning!
Elvenu nun!
Bother.

Aŭ ni bruligas vian arbon!
How in the sweaty hell does our boy suddenly speak Blue?
It's just a translation app, Paw.

Real question is, how's he getting reception out here when I can't get it in our own gee-damn dining room?

Please, take whatever you want.
Just don't hurt my home.

I'm not going to put up a fight.

Lord.
Never seen one of them up close before.

Enjoy.

UHN!
Kidd!

You filthy cunny!
SHOOM

Gross!

Our dear child still breathing?
Just got his bell rung.
Boy's dragon-hide coat took most of the brunt.

hngh
We know you ain't out here by your lonesome, longhorn.
Tell us who you're with and exactly what they got of worth...

...or we hang you from your own tree.
When did you first know that you'd give up your life for someone?

Okay, maybe you've never felt that way, but parents usually say that about their offspring, right?
KSSSSSSS

Personally, I think it's almost always a dumb idea to sacrifice your own existence for others.

Or worse, for some "cause."

If we were all a little more selfish with our own lives instead of being in such a hurry to defend everything to the death...
I can't fall asleep.

...the universe would be a much less scary place.
Will you sing me a song?

Marko.
Marko, am I dreaming?
Mmn?

Well, ***I*** was.
I have this recurring nightmare about my teeth climbing out of my head and turning into little...

...kiu?
So this ***isn't*** me having a psychotic break.

Alana, who... who is this boy?
It's me, Daddy.
It's ***Kurti.***

You know how to Forecast?!
I don't even know what that means!

It's a... a very powerful projection spell.
Our High Clerics use it to ***simulate*** long-term outcomes before going into battle.

That tickles!
This is your vision of the future.
A possible one, anyway.

Except it isn't.
That might be what I'd ***hoped*** for, but our baby is --
Holy smokes.

Is that a nice ghost?
Like Izabel?

Or a scary ghost?
Like from the creepy book cover I'm not supposed to look at before bed?

I'm not a ghost, ding dong.
I'm your favoritest brother.
Scary ghost.
He isn't dangerous, sweetheart.
He may be to you, love.
Every spell has a cost, and this one is particularly expensive. Forecasting hurts the *heart*.

No shit.

You don't understand. The longer you keep this enchantment going, the more you risk *cardiac arrest*.
But, I don't know how to make it stop.
And even if I did...

...how could I?

khh
No sense playin' noble.
Whoever your friends are, I guarantee they'd give **you** up before drawing their last.

...swear... I'm here... **alone**...
Bull. Your hooves are big, but not big enough to fill the fancy footwear we followed here. There's at least one man with you, a man with **money**.
Where's your whoremonger off to, harlot?

She's not going to spill, y'all.
Just snap her neck already.

...please...
...please don't hurt... my **dear child**...

Come again?
The bastard who knocked me up... demanded I get an ***abortion***.
Said the doctors out in your Badlands would take care of my kind, no questions asked.

But when I got here, I... I just couldn't go through with it.

Second I told my boyfriend, he said we were finished.
Haven't seen him since... but if you find the son of a bitch, I hope you rob him blind.
Heh.

You made the right call, not going to the Badlands.
Your baby ***and*** you would have been slaughtered soon as you got there.
What... what do you mean?

That place is run by ***monsters***.
And that ain't a figure of speech.

This looks fun!

Race you to the front door, Hazy?
Don't call me that.
And I'm real fast, so don't cry when I beat you!

I can't do this.

You're stronger than you think, love.
I think I'm plenty fucking strong, thanks.
I mean I can't do this to *Hazel*.

All she wants is for her mother to be healthy.
Maybe.
But after this... operation, I'm going to lose my awesome new superpowers, aren't I?
And that means we're going to lose *him*.
Again.

Alana, that is *not* our son.
Obviously.
He's everything I *thought* having a child would be... not the messy, beautiful reality.
But how do we explain that to *her*?

No fair!
I haven't learned to fly yet!

Can I ask you something?
What do you like best about being... you know... *alive*?

I dunno.
It's mostly boring, but then sometimes it's scary, which is way worse than the times when it's boring, so --

PBFFFFFFT

That.
Fart.
Was.
GREAT.

I know it's only temporary, but you let our girl learn who her little brother might have been.
That is a ***gift***.
If introducing her to people she's just going to lose is a gift... I'm worried we're starting to ***spoil*** the kid.

Hazel is shockingly resilient, like all children.
The more loss she experiences now, the stronger she'll --
hngh

Alana?

Uh-oh.

Mommy...?

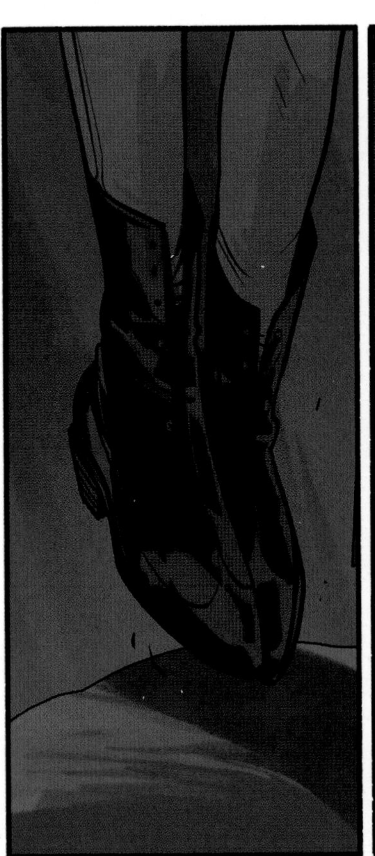

We don't want to hurt you *or* your unborn, miss.
Matter of fact, you tell us which way your rich ex ran off, we might be able to do you a kindness.
You're... you're going to kill him, aren't you?

Only if he puts up a fight.
But you said yourself, the man is a scoundrel.

Don't be shy.
We're doing this for the good of you *and* your bundle of --

HRAH!

NGH!

NAAAAAH!

HELL-
BITCH!

ptoo

...not afraid -hkk- to die...
...just wanted to -kkh- spite her ugly face first...
We're gonna end you **twice** for that, you vicious --

GAHH!

When it comes to life-or-death situations, I'm a big fan of the "live to fight another day" strategy.
Evening.

The first half of that plan, anyway.
Just stopped by to return a few things.
D. OSWALD
HEIST
PETITE DEATH
III

But "live to sleep past another noon" doesn't sound nearly as inspiring.

What's wrong with Mommy?
Why aren't you helping her?!
I... I can't.

We need to **shock** her heart awake.
But I only know how to cast ***lightning,*** and that much current would kill your mother for sure.

Which is why ***you*** have to help her.
What?!

Just... just please listen to me, Hazel. Please listen.
Someone your age will create much less current than an old man like me. All you have to do is, is spell *fulmo*.
I don't know how!

You know what doubt is, don't you?
Kinda?
Good, that's good, because this incantation is fueled by ***doubt***.

Everyone feels it, even Mommy and Daddy.
Doubt can paralyze you, can... can make you not want to do anything.

But if you learn to ***channel*** it, to turn those feelings away from yourself and out at the world...

...you can doubt what's impossible.

F...
U... L...
M...

O!
KRAKOOM

HWUH

Sorry, sorry, sorry!
Don't be, honey girl.
You just saved our family.

But we still have to get your mother to a *professional*...
YES YES YES, MY DARLINGS.

YOU'RE IN SUCH VERY GOOD HANDS.

end chapter forty-five

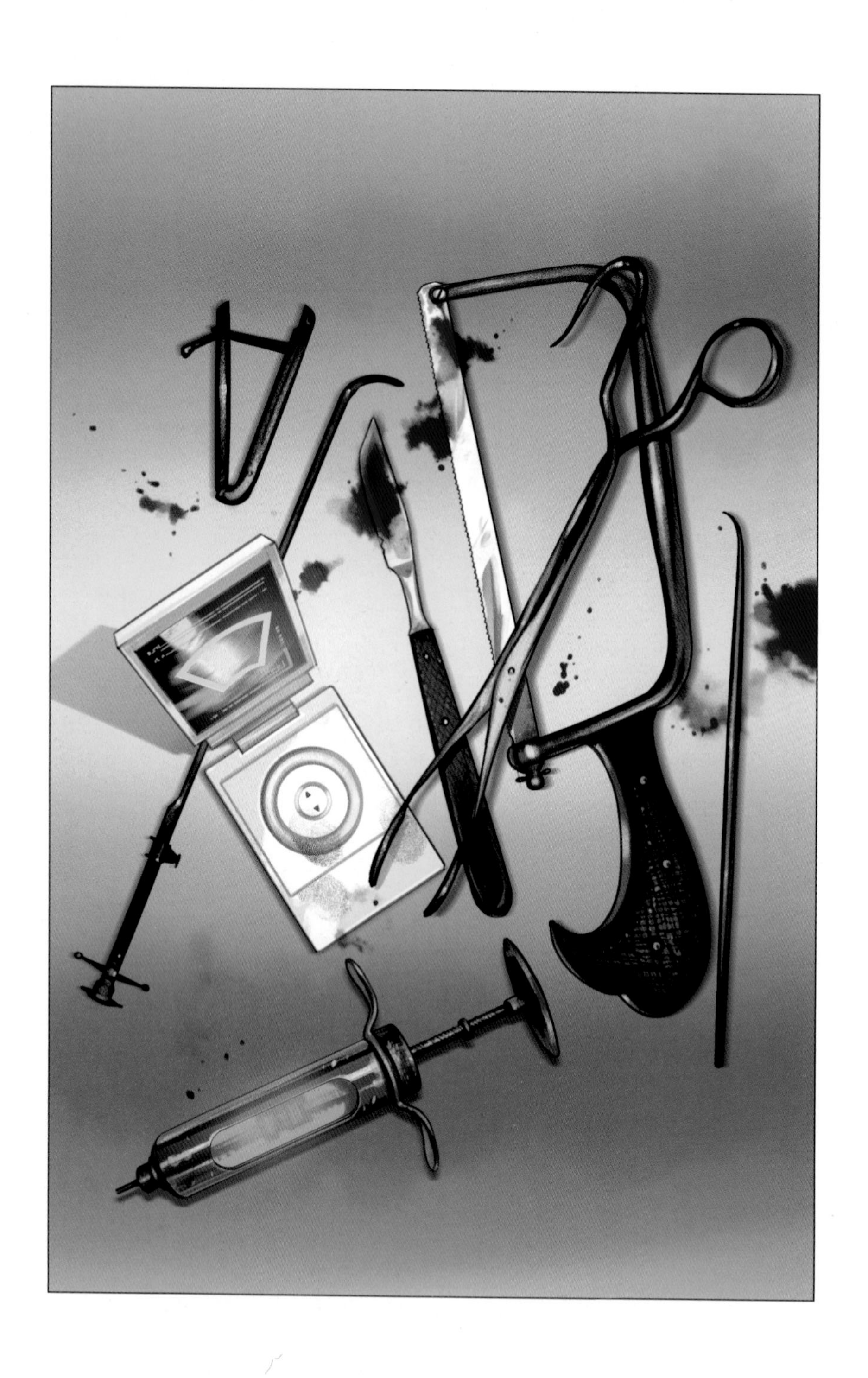

CHAPTER

FORTY-SIX

Pease!
Wee suffhurr ennuh!

We're beggin' you, sir.
Kindly show a little **mercy.**

Fuck your mercy in the face.
-koff- -koff- -koff-

You ignorant hayseeds thought you could *lynch* an innocent woman?
Woman? Sir, she's just a *Wreather*.
I... I was thinking her kind was your mortal enemy.

Yes.
Well.

Kill Maw and me if you have to.
S'pose we got it coming.

But won't you please spare our darling son?

Son...?

I ain't a child, Paw.
I'm as ready to meet our Maker as --
Shut your mouth when the adults are speaking, gelding.

You arseholes aren't worth the shallow graves I'd have to dig for your corpses.
Go on, get the hell out of my sight.

But set foot around these parts again, I turn your entire family to ***glue***.

...what...?

Yes, yes.
"This ain't over," etcetera.

You all right, Petrichor?
Not too late for me to shoot those animals in their backs if you'd --

Drone piece of ***SHIT!***

Would you care to repeat that?

Fuck your white knight act!
I didn't need you to save me!
That hemp necklace tells a different story, you ungrateful moony slag!

If it weren't for my timely intervention, you'd be a goddamn **bird feeder** right now.
No kidding, Robot.

But you just had to go and ruin a good thing.
My parents taught me never to get too attached to new people who came into my life, since attachment is the root of suffering.

But the times I've suffered most were when I had NO attachments, so who knows, right?
COME COME COME.
BRING YOUR LOVED ONE TO ME.

Stay the hell away from my family.

AHH, YES, WHAT SIGHT I MUST BE!
APOLOGIES, HAVE NOT YET HAD CHANCE TO SCRUB OUT SINCE HELPING MY LAST PATIENT.
Are you a doctor-lady?

OF SORT.
I AM *ENDWIFE*, AND I AM HERE TO HELP THOSE IN NEED.

At what cost?
MY SERVICES ARE PROVIDED ON... SLIDING SCALE.
IF YOU HAVE NO MONEY, PERHAPS YOU MAY REPAY WITH FAVOR ANOTHER DAY?

BUT LET US DISCUSS SUCH MATTERS LATER, FATHER.
FOR MOMENT, MOTHER APPEARS IN DIRE WAY, SO WHAT CHOICE DO YOU HAVE BUT TO COME INTO MY HOME?

NO CHOICE AT ALL, I THINK.

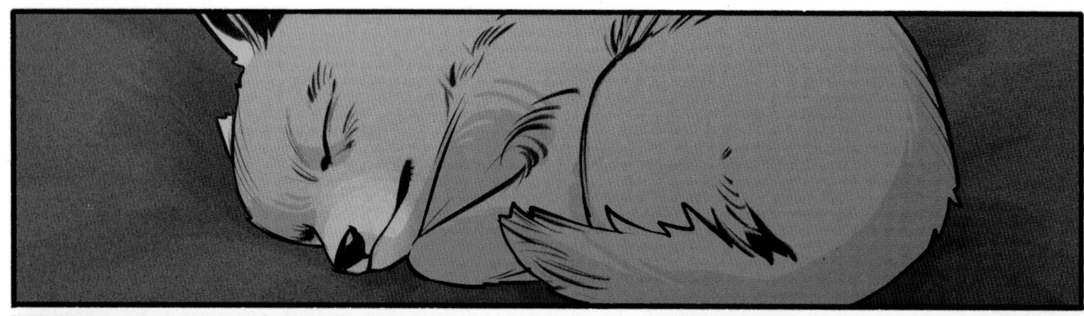

PAY NO MIND TO MY PUPS. THEIR BELLIES ARE FULL SO THEY WILL SLEEP UNTIL MORNING.
YOU TWO MAY WAIT WITH THEM WHILE I ATTEND TO MOTHER.

I won't leave Alana's side, Endwife.
MRRRN.
VERY WELL, YOU MAY JOIN ME IN MY THEATER...

...BUT I DO NOT THINK YOUR TREASURED ONE WILL WANT TO SEE WHAT COMES NEXT.

Stay here, Hazel.
I promise I'll be right back and Mommy will be all better, okay?
Okay.

Big sister?
Ahh!

Are you as afraid as I am?

Uh-uh, imaginary brother.

I'm not afraid at all.

What in fuck's name does someone like you have to be *suicidal* about?
If you really wanted to top yourself, you should have done it when you were a bloody P.O.W., not as a newly free woman.
You call this free?

At least Alana hasn't ***banished*** you.
After she returns, I'm sure her family will take you wherever the hell you want to be.
Like Wreath? There's nothing there for me anymore.
My own family no longer speaks to me, and the man I loved left his heart on the battlefield... along with most of his other vital organs.

Ah.
I suppose my Coalition was responsible?
No, just another hapless victim of *"friendly fire."*

Yes, my dear wife was killed by one of my own.
Frankly, it was easier to lose people I cared about to ***your lot***. At least I knew where to channel some of the old bottomless rage.

Spare me your false empathy, Robot.
You have ***no clue*** what that man meant to me. Flustro was the only person who stood by my side during an unimaginably challenging... transition.
No need to be coy, Petrichor.

I am well aware of your "*secret identity.*"

How? Did Hazel --
No, and I'm sure her myopic parents are still in the dark. I, however, had a sense from the moment we first met.
Between us, I have always been rather...

...fluid.

Bully for you.
But the universe isn't as easy to navigate for those of us who weren't fortunate enough to be born into ***royalty***.
If you say so.

By the by, what the hell kind of lethal potion are you concocting over there?
Viskio.
Back in prison, one of the girls taught us how to turn bug guts into ***rotgut***.

Alcohol?
Blessed, life-giving alcohol?

Not exactly top shelf, but it'll sauté your brain, which is all I'm after.

Care for a nip before you're on your way?
...twist my arm.

To old friends and new enemies.
Chin-fucking-chin.

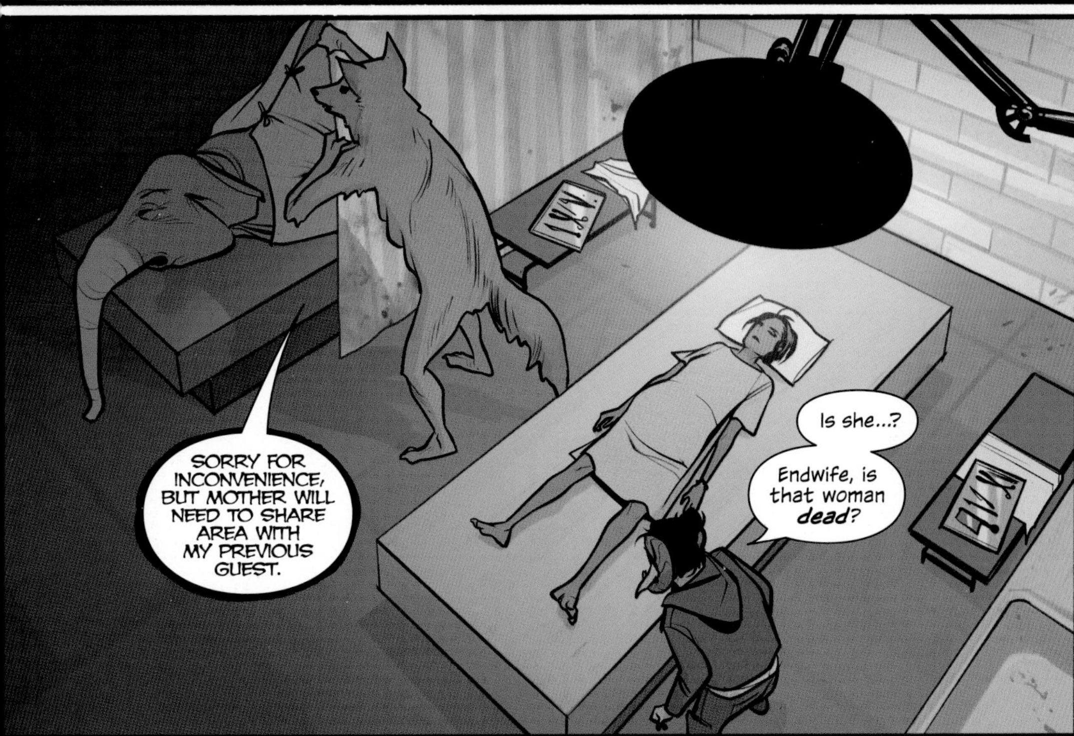
SORRY FOR INCONVENIENCE, BUT MOTHER WILL NEED TO SHARE AREA WITH MY PREVIOUS GUEST.
Is she...?
Endwife, is that woman *dead*?

FOR COUPLE WITH GREAT NEED FOR PRIVACY, YOU ARE MOST CAVALIER ABOUT PATIENT CONFIDENTIALITY.
Forgive me, I only --
AM JUST HAVING FUN WITH YOU, HORNED ONE. IS CLEAR YOU AND YOUR WINGED WIFE ARE VERY GOOD AT KEEPING SECRETS, YES?

THE WOMAN YOU SAW IS MERELY RECUPERATING.
REMOVING A VIABLE FETUS AT THIRTY WEEKS CAN BE MOST CHALLENGING OPERATION.
Thirty *weeks*?

IS THERE PROBLEM?
It's just, I remember how strong Hazel's **kicks** felt around then.
She probably could have survived out of the womb by that age...

AHH, SO YOU DISAPPROVE OF WORK I DO HERE.
I'm eternally grateful for however you can help my wife, ma'am.
But I'd be lying if I said I didn't have misgivings about this place. I mean, Alana's fetus -- our **child** -- has already passed, but other babies...

My father wasn't particularly religious, but I guess you could say he considered himself *"pro-life."*
And not just when it came to abortion. He raised me to be against things like capital punishment, even eating meat.

AND YET, AM I WRONG WHEN I SENSE YOU COME FROM LONG LINE OF SOLDIERS?
Dad felt that a *"just war"* was sometimes a necessary evil, but I'm no longer sure there **is** such a thing.
I choose to believe that the taking of any life should always be avoided.

MMN, IDEOLOGIES ARE LOVELY... BUT DOWN HERE, IS ONLY REALITY.

Whose reality?
I can't imagine **every** woman who comes to you only does so because her own life is in danger.
NO, LIKE MOST, MY LAST PATIENT COULD HAVE EASILY CARRIED HER CHILD TO TERM.

BUT ONLY DAYS AGO, DOCTOR WAS ABLE TO DETECT THAT HER UNBORN HAD DEVELOPED MOST TERRIBLE BRAIN DEFECT.
HER LITTLE ONE MAY HAVE SURVIVED, BUT THERE IS NO QUESTION THE CHILD'S LIFE WOULD BE SHORT AND PAINFUL.

TELL ME, FATHER.
WHAT WOULD YOU AND BEAUTIFUL BRIDE HAVE DONE WITH SUCH NEWS?

MMN.
PASS FORCEPS, WILL YOU, PLEASE?

If they really fix Mama, am I gonna get deaded?

It's *die.*
And I don't know if somebody who's make-believe can even do that.
I'm not make-believe, I'm Kurti!

No, Kurti was a friend of mine who died for real.
I don't wanna hurt your feelings, but Daddy says you're more like... like an *idea.*

Can an idea get deaded?
Die.
And I don't think so, long as somebody remembers it.

Will you remember me, Hazel? Forever and ever?
Maybe... but I can't cross my heart.
I liked the other Kurti a whole lot, but I already have trouble remembering what color eyes he had and stuff.

Oh.
Then, before I go, will you at least sing me a song?

I'm... not that good a singer.
That's okay.
Do you know any lullabies?

The only ones I know were made up by my old babysitter.
Izabel.

She died, too.
Again.

I'm real sorry.
But, do you remember how any of her songs went?
...

Good night, chubby baby
I can't rock you no more
I'm sorry, chubby baby
But my arms are getting sore
Sleep tight, chubby baby
And please don't get me wrong
You're a perfect sized baby
So never accept fakey beauty standards or develop unhealthy body issues...

...from this dumb song
Heh.
"Dumb."

That sounded real awesome, Hazy.
Thanks.
Can't believe I still know the whole thing.
You should totally be a *singer* when you grow up.
...I don't know.
My parents say I'm probably gonna be a doctor or something.

Mommy and Daddy are wrong.
You're gonna be the bestest singer ever.

Goodbye, Hazel.

Goodbye, baby brother.
It's funny which random moments from the past our minds choose to cling to, isn't it?

Okay, maybe more interesting than funny, but still...
PETITE DEATHS III
You've been hacking your way through these trashy romance novels, too?
Only for lack of less boring options.
I gather the lovebirds grabbed every D. Oswald Heist book they could find before fleeing the author's home.
I just wish Marko and Alana had become obsessed with someone who knew how to write proper action.
Hell, I'd settle for an epic poem from one of your old masters.
Hold on, you know the works of the Robot Kingdom?
When I was a student, I read some of your ancient war stories... from back when your fickle world was still an ally of our moon.
Before you bastards betrayed us and sided with the wings.
Oh, please.
You're the ones who backstabbed my people centuries ago.
If you say so.

I *do* say so, you mouthy trollop.
I knew it was a bad idea to share a drink with your kind.
There's too much history between us.

History?
I barely even know you!
Clearly, you conceited fop.

Are you looking to start something, Petrichor?
Make a move and find out, Robot.

I promise you will come to regret those words.

One way to find out, bitch.

end chapter forty-six

CHAPTER FORTY-SEVEN

BILLY!

Sophie?
Help!

He's gonna kill me!
You'll wish I did.
Now fetch me a **proper** switch to use on your deceitful ass.

Dad.
St... st... **stop it**.

Fuh... fuh... **fuck off**, Bill.
Your sister's a willful brat who needs to learn some --

thwap

That's enough of that.

Good to see you, pal.
But if you please, while I'm on the clock, I go by *The Letter*.
Uncle Steve.

The hell is this, **Steve**?
Your worthless drunk sister hire you to shake me down for alimony?
Angie's a year sober. Got her old job back and everything.
All she wants is to be a mother again.
So I'm here to take the children home.

Home? Some leaky-ass **fishing boat**?
If you think I'm letting my flesh and blood go **anywhere,** you're out of your --
Sophie sent us a letter.

About what you get up to in that cabin of yours.

Sorry.

You oughtn't have done that.

Don't, Steve!
Don't you even --

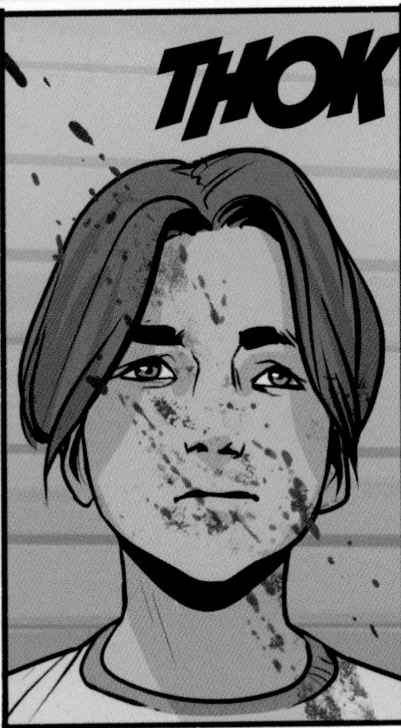
THOK

Damn, look how crisp that blood looks on your adorable psycho cheeks!

This magic VCR cost more than my first apartment, but it was *so* worth it.

Sweet Boy...?

Oh, yeah, after I shot you, I had your dog turned into a *rug!*
How's that for some super-villain shit?
...why...?

Because you murdered the man I was going to *marry*, you fat fuck.
My name's *Ianthe*, and while I look forward to eventually decapitating you, I thought it might be more fun to make you watch me kill all your loved ones first.

But it looks like you've already managed to lose most of your family, so we'll have to fast-forward through some more shitty memories to find other contenders.
FREELANCER KILLED WHILE VISITING DEMIMONDE
koff listen to me koff
I did something to your kin back when I was The Will, you got every right to end me... but you start offing civilians, the Constables are gonna give you the chair.
Except they won't, you complete asshole.
I could burn down a nursing home and never even spend a night in lockup.
...you some kinda made woman?
Better.
I'm a diplomat.
That's just another word for gangster.
No, it's another word for gangster with immunity.
Long as I give my home world the occasional intel about which side of the war they should help fund this month, I can do pretty much whatever the fuck I want.
And my newest hobby is binge-watching this misery.
HNNNGH!

I'm thinking about getting a Sidekick.

Ugh, so predictable.
That's what **every** Freelancer going through a midlife crisis does.
I ain't middle-aged.

This line of work, we're **both** over the hill.

Whatever, Stalk.
Unlike you, I could use an extra pair of eyes.
Just don't get something that sheds.
Why do you even care?
We almost never work the same jobs these days.
Yeah, but if I ever spend the night at your place, I don't want disgusting hair getting all over my nice clothes.
You own clothes?
Plural?

Har har.
I love that you ding that but don't even *react* to the suggestion of me spending the night.
Who gives a shit if you need to crash with me sometime?

Because I'm not talking about a grade-school sleepover, dummy.
I'm talking about *sexytimes*.

Call it that again, and we're never sleeping in the same *orbit*, much less --
I GIVE UP!

The hostage! The hostage you're looking for, she's down on P3!
She's alive. She's alive, I swear. And I surrender. I surrender unconditionally.

I'm begging you, I only took this job to take care of my mom.
I did it for the money, and the money *blows*.

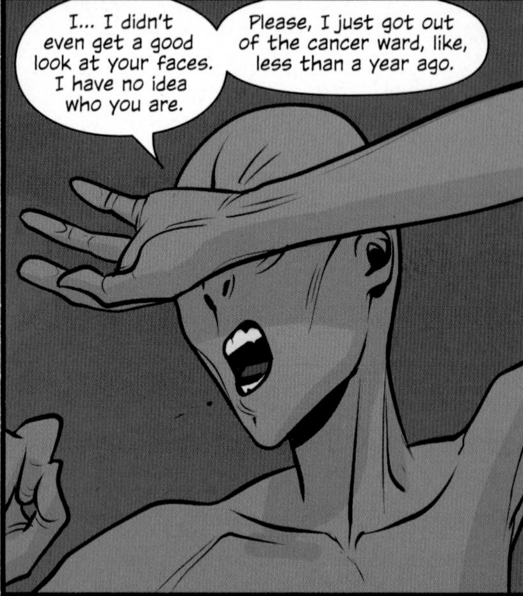
I... I didn't even get a good look at your faces. I have no idea who you are.
Please, I just got out of the cancer ward, like, less than a year ago.

Plus, I finally met someone.
I met someone and I think she might actually --

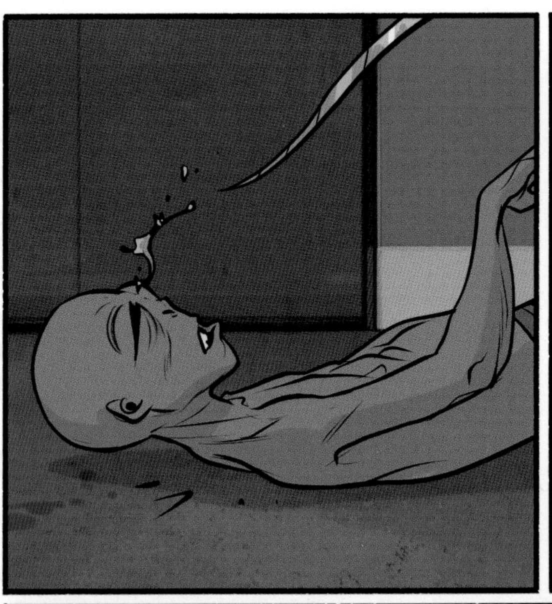

Who knows if he was even telling the truth?

And I'm not doing much later.
If you want to come over, I mean.

Okay.

Boo!
Fucking filler!

You're telling me this chick gets killed in action, too?
Does *everyone* you meet end up dead?

You'll see.

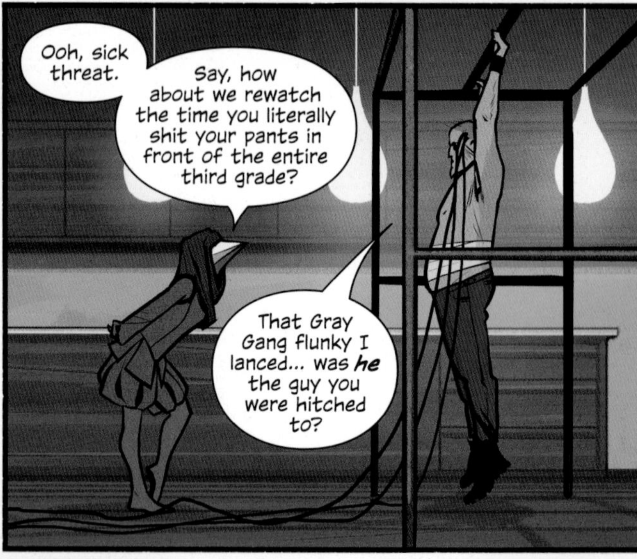
Ooh, sick threat.
Say, how about we rewatch the time you literally shit your pants in front of the entire third grade?
That Gray Gang flunky I lanced... was *he* the guy you were hitched to?

Well now.
I was going to save this dramatic reveal until we caught up to the actual moment of his death, but all right, what the hell?

Years ago, I was engaged to a young man named *Hektor*. One fine day he visited the planet Indica for work...
...and you cut his face in half.

But it used to be pretty as mine.
Sorry.
Not ringing any bells.
Are... are you fucking kidding me?
He was a private security consultant, helping his brothers on some case for Sextillion. You ***butchered*** all three of them.
Oh. Yeah. Mama Sun's goons, right?

Lady, your boyfriend was working for a bunch of kid rapists.
Wish I could kill him again.

You're a goddamn *liar*. Hektor was no angel, but he'd never have any part of... of hurting a child.
Keep watching.
Enjoy the show.

Fuck your moralizing. Do you have any idea how many young people I've watched you *execute*?
Whatever kind of bastards happened to be cutting a check to my fiancé, he didn't deserve what you did to him.

Maybe he was just another random hash mark to you, but Hektor was the only man in my fucked-up life who made me *laugh*.
I don't know if a woman has ever done that for you, but if so, we're going to find her.

And I'm going to feed you her severed cunt.

Excuse me.

Shit!
Sorry, Gwendolyn.
Relax, my people aren't as hung up as you prudes about nipples.

All the same, I didn't even see nothing.
LYING

Do me a favor and scram, will you?

May I ask something?
Where in the fuck did you even find such a creature?

Lying Cat?
Bought her at a pet store in some ratty old mall.
Bullshit.

Everyone told me to go to one of those "rescue" shelters, but most of those animals are straight psycho.
...
I can't tell whether or not you're messing with me, Will.

Anyway, just a heads-up that the repair guys are finally here.
Should be able to get my ship patched in a few hours.
Tell them we'll pay double for a **rush job.**

I know you don't believe me, but this is about much more than Marko.
Now **you** relax.
Settling the score with your pervert ex is gonna take as long as it takes.

His mongrel child is nothing less than a time bomb.
If the general population ever learns that a Wreath Foot Soldier willingly **procreated** with an enlisted Landfallian woman --
Uhhhm, bitch, ***rewind.***

Ianthe, please.

Please don't hurt her.
Her?
Billy Boy, if what tits here says is true, I'll be rich enough to hunt down and torture everyone you've ever even **met**.

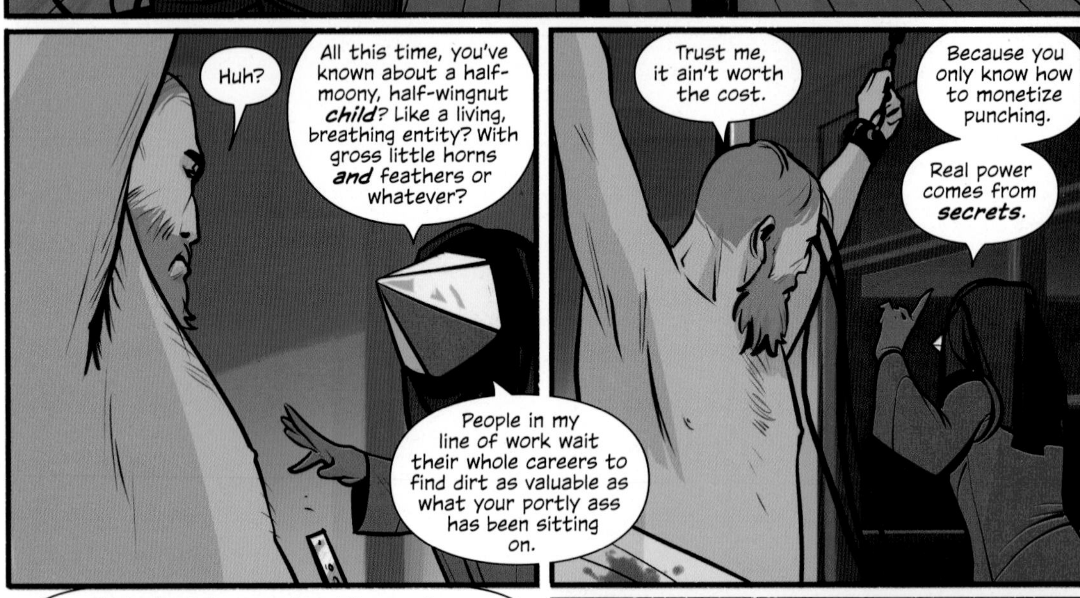
Huh?
All this time, you've known about a half-moony, half-wingnut **child**? Like a living, breathing entity? With gross little horns **and** feathers or whatever?
People in my line of work wait their whole careers to find dirt as valuable as what your portly ass has been sitting on.
Trust me, it ain't worth the cost.
Because you only know how to monetize punching.
Real power comes from **secrets**.

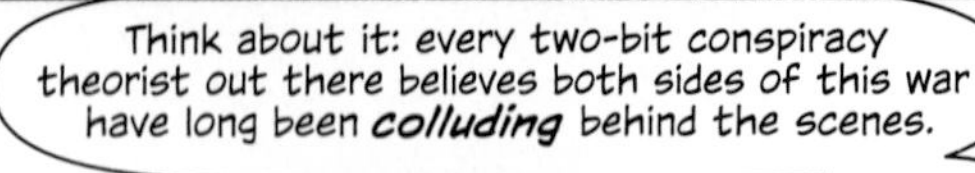
Think about it: every two-bit conspiracy theorist out there believes both sides of this war have long been **colluding** behind the scenes.

But if your bloated head contains proof that a couple of their soldiers are **literally** in bed together...

...I can crack the fucking universe in half.

But we have to haul ass.
What's this "we" crap?
Best finish your revenging now, 'cause I'm not going ***anywhere*** with you.

Oh, Bill.
You profoundly stupid person.

We're already on our way.
NAHHH!

You know, I'm almost grateful Hektor brought you into my life.
AHHHH!

We're going to do something right with everything you've done wrong.

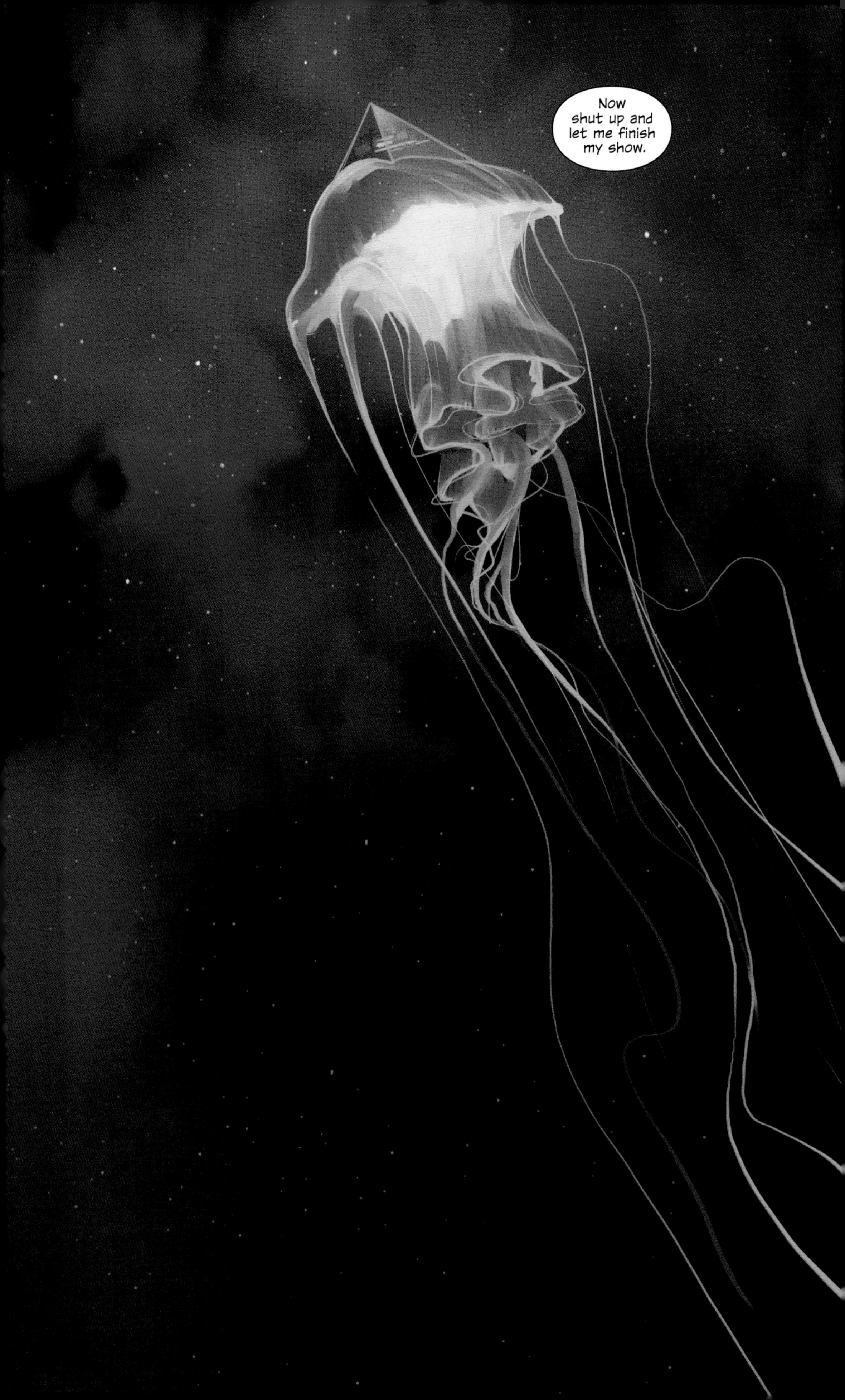
Now shut up and let me finish my show.

end chapter forty-seven

CHAPTER FORTY-EIGHT

I'm sorry you had to see this.

Don't you dare, Mister Upsher.
Don't you dare hurt one hair on that girl's head.

It's not a girl, it's an animal!
And I'll be goddamned if we let *actual people* starve to death while what's left of this blubber rots!
I'm hungry as you are, but Ghüs knows we just gotta hold out hope that Marko and Alana and their rocketful of food will be back real soon.

You've been saying that for *months!*
I'm sorry, but much as I'd kill to interview your freaky friends, you have to accept that they're *never* coming back to this blighted shitstain.

Face it, those fugitive lovebirds are *dead*... like my boyfriend's going to be if we don't get him something more to eat than wilted fucking crops.
...too much smoke... in the darkroom...

What if we slayed a Dread Naught?

The hell is that?
A wild thing, big game with plenty of meat on its bones.
Heard one howling a few weeks back.

Then why in god's name haven't you hunted it down yet?!
'Cause the tricky beast is *invisible*, least until the day it dies.

Not to my kind.
We can see their *insides*.
Now how do you know that, Squire?

Because I saw one last night.
In the Barrens.

Gosh darn it!
How many times has Ghüs told you *never* to go in those woods?
You actually believe *anything* this little sneak says?

Yesterday, I caught him stealing from Doff's share of the rations.
On my oath, he... he *gave* me those berries!
Enough.

Gimme one night to see if I can make a meal out of Squire's monster.

If I don't catch nothing... then I'll carve up sweet Friendo myself.
RRRMMM

Of course, I shall be joining you.
Don't want to hear it, son.
Swore to Sir Robot I'd keep you safe until he got back, and the thing we're after is a *killer*.

I've spotted the Dread Naught once, and I can spot it again.
Besides, I'm safer with you than I am with the newspaperman and his picture-maker.
He's not wrong.
If the fat-ass Freelancer who stranded us here ever comes back, it'll be to finish making that kid pay for his father's sins.
...don't have... The Will...
Hmf.
You gotta promise to do *whatever* Ghüs tells you.
I vow on the soul of my late mother.

Then fetch your weapon already.
One day, a boy decided to break the rules.

Like in most children's stories, he then had an adventure.
This experience taught the boy that those aforementioned rules were there for a reason.
But he also learned another important lesson... that one should break rules as often as possible.
Because who the hell doesn't want to have an adventure?
Have you ever killed someone?

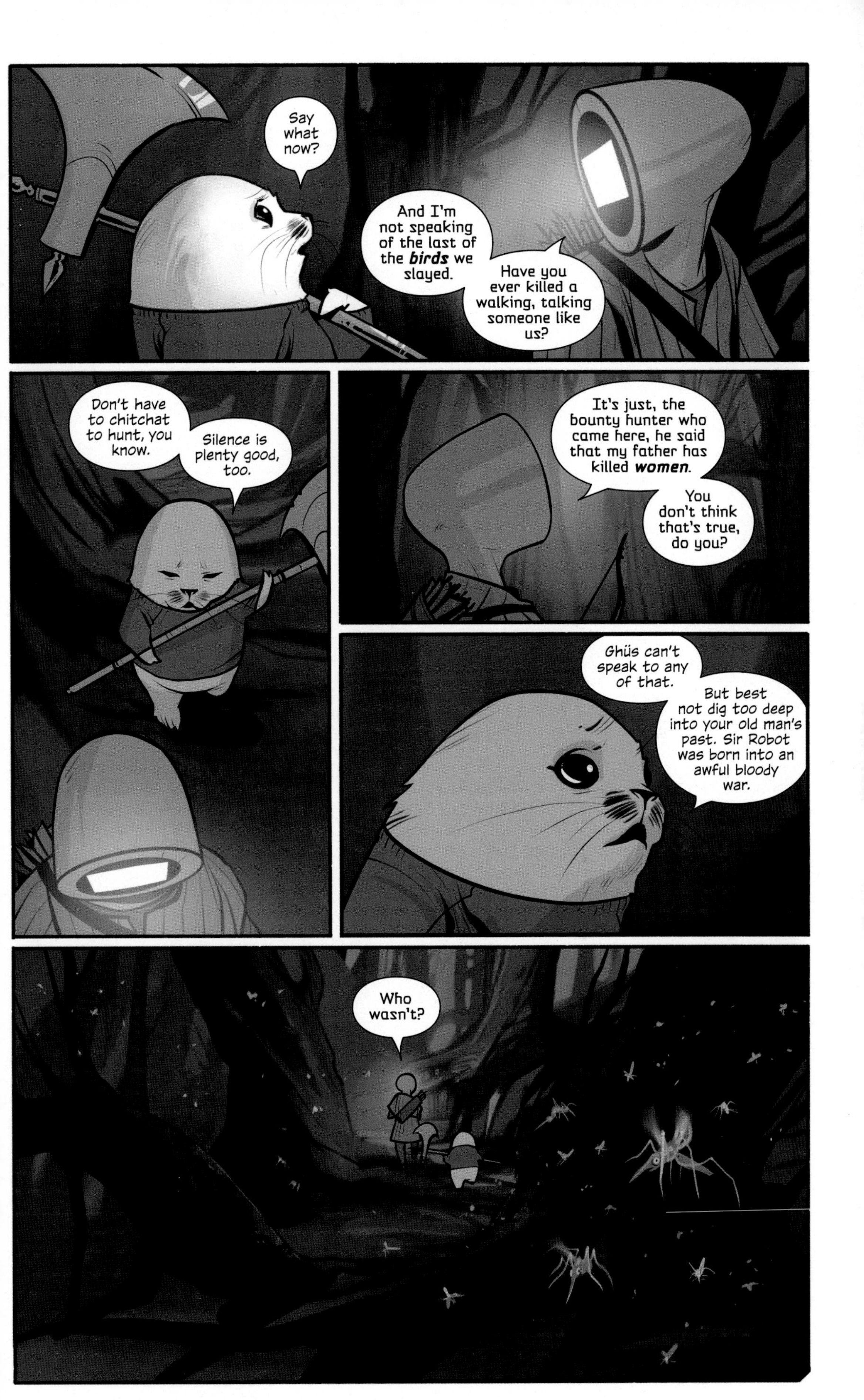
Say what now?
And I'm not speaking of the last of the *birds* we slayed.
Have you ever killed a walking, talking someone like us?
Don't have to chitchat to hunt, you know.
Silence is plenty good, too.
It's just, the bounty hunter who came here, he said that my father has killed *women*.
You don't think that's true, do you?
Ghüs can't speak to any of that.
But best not dig too deep into your old man's past. Sir Robot was born into an awful bloody war.
Who wasn't?

I suppose.
Either way, bad things need doing when folks are at war.
Don't matter if you're a he or a she or what have you.
OW
Sometimes, killing is the only thing to be done.

Did you see that?
A shooting star!
No such thing.

But, I saw it with my own eyes!
Maybe, but it ain't a star.
Just a clump of space dirt catching fire.

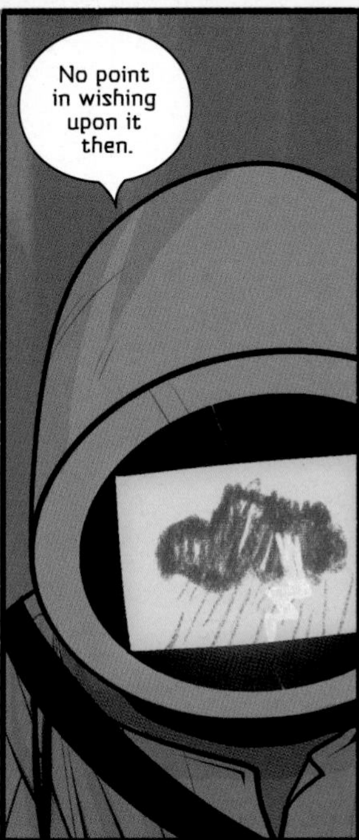
No point in wishing upon it then.

Aw, don't listen to Ghüs, little fella. I'm just tired and hungry.
No, you're quite right.
I'm all alone in this universe, and nothing in the heavens will change that.

But I'll never marry a beautiful princess like my father did.
Don't you talk like that.
No matter what, Ghüs will always be there for you.
Father says a true knight's most important duty is to his romantic partner.
But so long as we're unwelcome in the Robot Kingdom, I can't even visit the one world where my courtly love might be.
Aren't you a little young to be worrying about that kinda stuff?
Well, for what it's worth, I don't think folks gotta get *hitched* to be happy.
Ol' Ghüs has always kept his own company just fine.
Then why go to all this trouble just to spare your *pet*?
Friendo is a lot more than that to me.
You mean, you and the walrus... lie together?

Huh?!
No, geez, nothing like that!

I mean, my people, we got a strong bond with all our livestock, but there was always something special about Friendo.
Ah.
Got her from my **sister**, after she passed from the lung disease.

Wasn't a very good brother to her, never called enough or nothing.
But when I look into her animal's eyes, it's almost like...

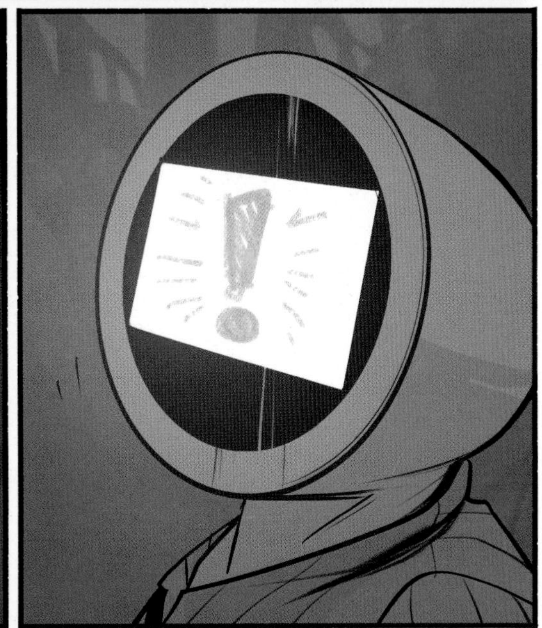
!

Squire?

You okay?

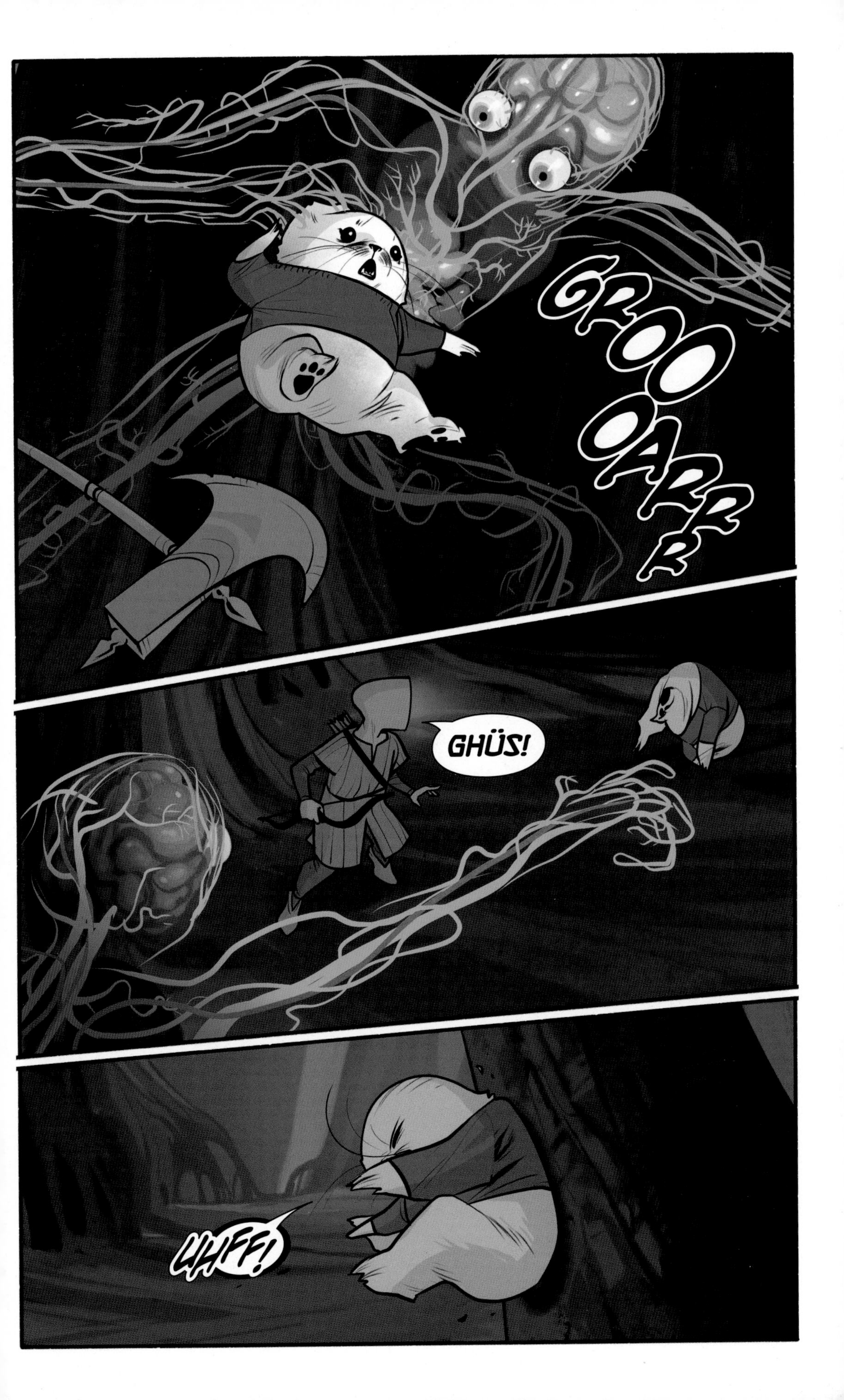
GROOOARRR
GHÜS!
UHFF!

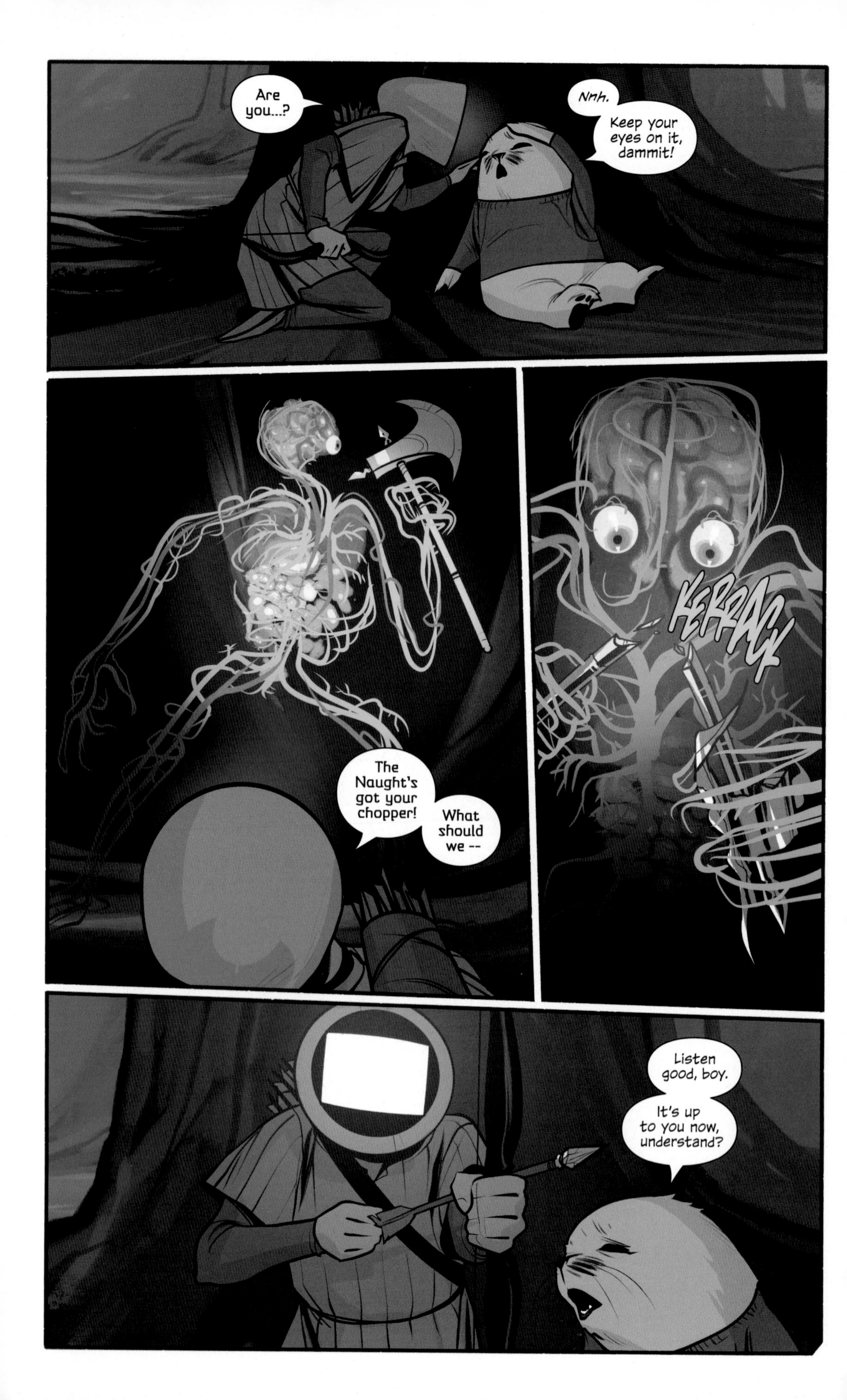

Are you...?
Nnh.
Keep your eyes on it, dammit!
The Naught's got your chopper!
What should we --
KERRACK
Listen good, boy.
It's up to you now, understand?

HRRRGH
That's it!
Your aim looks true!
All you gotta do is *let go!*

I cannot.

What are you doing?!
Don't look away! You'll let it...

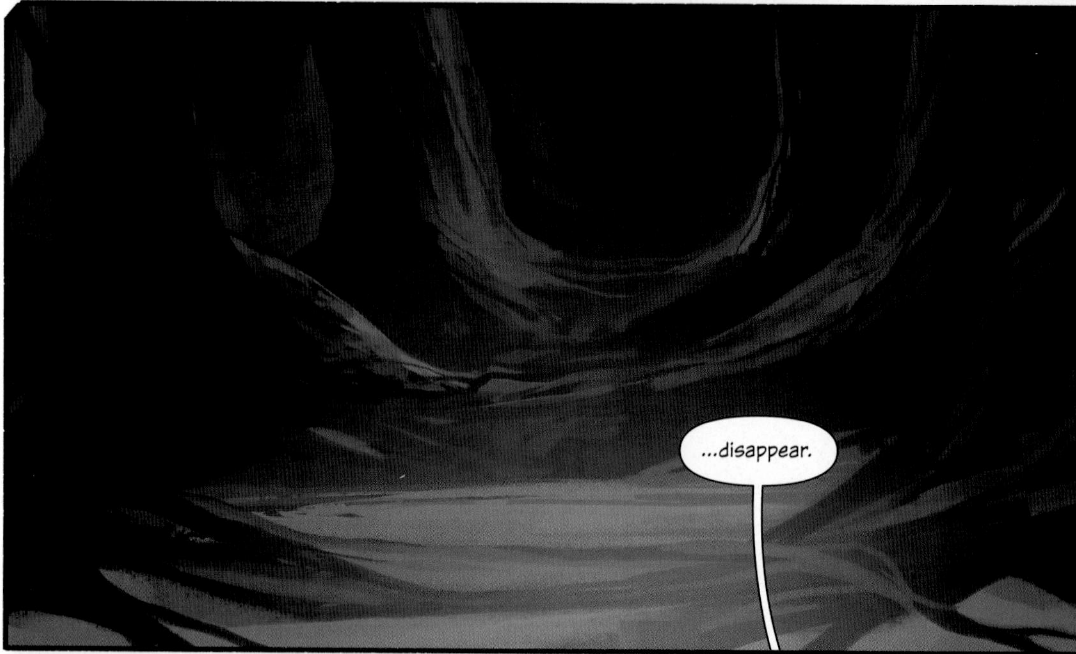
...disappear.

Forgive me.
I... I thought I could slay it, but --
You did your best, Squire.

And that'll have to do.

Ghüs...
I told you, I'm not cross.
Just sad about what's gotta happen next.
No, look.
Is that **smoke** coming from our grounds?
I'll be darned.
You don't think they cooked Friendo already, do you?
What we saw in the sky last night.
That weren't a shooting star **or** space dirt.
It was them.

Squire?

Papa.

Welcome back from your quest, Sir Robot.
On your bloody feet, young man.
Let's see how much you've grown.

My word.

It is... it is **very good** to see you again, lad.
Yes.
It is very good to see you, as well.

I only wish I could have returned sooner.
Our journey was a complicated one, but I owe a tremendous debt to my new friend Petrichor for persuading --
Why aren't you **hugging** him?

Boys are weird.
Be nice, dear.
Though you're not wrong.

Squire, it is my great honor to introduce you to Marko and Alana's daughter ***Hazel***.
That's her?
The fair maiden?

You don't ***look*** like a fair maiden.
So what?
Do you even know what a fidget spinner is?

Of course I do.
Then what does one look like?

I have no idea what a fidget spinner is.

Come on, squirt.
I'll show you.
One day, a boy decided to break the rules.

And that boy would
become my brother.

to be continued

Fiona's black-and-white and color artwork for *The Coffin*,

an incentive print for stores ordering the 25-cent Chapter Forty-Three.

TO BE CONTINUED IN
SAGA CHAPTER FORTY-NINE
ON SALE FEBRUARY 2018
AT YOUR LOCAL COMIC BOOK STORE AND ONLINE

BREAKING NEWS

WE'RE ALL COMPLETELY F